Give your child a head start with MUPPET™ PICTURE READERS

Starring the Muppets!

Kermit

Miss Piggy

Fozzie

Gonzo

Dear Parent,

Now children as young as preschool age can have the fun and satisfaction of reading a book all on their own.

In every Muppet Picture Reader, there are simple words, rebus pictures, and 24 flash cards to cut out and keep. (There is a flash card for every rebus picture plus extra cards for reading practice.) After children listen to each story a couple of times, they will be ready to try it all by themselves.

Collect all the titles in our Muppet Picture Reader series. Once children have mastered these books, they can move on to Levels 1, 2, and 3 in our All Aboard Reading series.

ISBN 0-448-41552-6 A B C D E F G H I J

A MUPPET™ PICTURE READER

Kermit's Teeny Tiny Farm

Written by Jennifer Dussling
Illustrated by Rick Brown

MUPPET PRESS
Grosset & Dunlap • New York

 ran

up a  .

 ran

across a

and down the  .

 was so happy.

He had a new farm.

ran by  .

 was putting

into the  .

"I have a new farm!

A little farm!"

 called to  .

"A farm! How great!"

 said.

"I will bring

a for the

in the 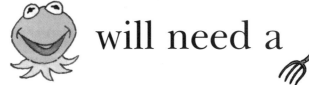.

will need a

on his farm."

ran by .

 was walking

her .

"I have a new farm!

A little farm!"

 called to .

"A farm!" said.

"I will bring

a  for the

that the  will lay.

 will need a

on his farm."

ran by .

 was riding

a  .

"I have a new farm!

A little farm!"

 called to  .

"A farm!"  said.

"I will bring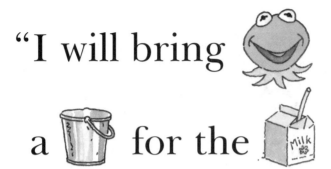

a for the Milk

that the will give.

will need a

on his farm."

ran to his .

Then  heard a

tap, tap, tap at the .

 opened the .

It was

and  and .

"Take us to the farm!"

they said.

"Here is a  for
the ," said.

"Here is a for
the ," said.

"Here is a for
the ," said.

"You are all very nice,"  said.

"But I do not need

a  or a

or a

for my little farm.

I will show you."

"Here is my little farm," said .

"It is an 🐜 farm!"

hill	Kermit
road	bridge
letter	Fozzie

pitchfork	mailbox
barn	hay
dog	Miss Piggy

eggs	basket
Gonzo	chicken
pail	bike

cow

milk

door

house

hat

ant